Evie's
Magic
Bracelet

Read more in the Evie's Magic Bracelet series!

Evie's Magic Bracelet

The Golden Sands

JESSICA ENNIS-HILL

and Elen Caldecott

**Illustrated by
Erica-Jane Waters**

Hodder
Children's
Books

HODDER CHILDREN'S BOOKS

First published in Great Britain in 2017 by Hodder and Stoughton

1 3 5 7 9 10 8 6 4 2

A CIP catalogue record for this book
is available from the British Library.

ISBN 978 1 444 93445 8

Printed and bound in Great Britain
by Clays Ltd, St Ives plc

The paper and board used in this book
are made from wood from responsible sources

Hodder Children's Books
An imprint of
Hachette Children's Group
Part of Hodder and Stoughton
Carmelite House
50 Victoria Embankment
London EC4Y 0DZ

An Hachette UK Company
www.hachette.co.uk

www.hachettechildrens.co.uk

To Mum and Dad
– J. E-H.

Peggy, finally
getting there
– E.C.

Chapter 1

Evie Hall sat on her suitcase and bounced like a bunny on springs. But the case was too full to shut. It didn't even come close. Perhaps there was something she might leave behind? She stood up sadly and lifted the lid. Inside she had clothes for sunny days, clothes for rainy days and clothes for snowy

days; boots, books and a boogie board;
spare bobbles, bobble hat, spare bobble hat.

Was it too much?

She could maybe leave the scarf and gloves
behind?

After all, the holiday was a week in Wales,
in the middle of summer.

Evie pulled out one or two things, hoping
for the best, when she heard Mum shout
from downstairs.

'Evie, the postie has a delivery for you!'

Evie dropped her scarf and gloves as
though they were scalding and raced out of
her attic bedroom.

It was always exciting when the postie had
a parcel for her, because there was always a

2

chance that he was bringing a present from Grandma Iris. Grandma Iris' presents were special – she sent bracelets that let Evie do magic for three whole days! Every one had led to a brilliant adventure. Was this another one? Just in time for the holiday?

Evie whizzed down the stairs and tumbled into the hall.

'Careful!' Mum laughed. There were already bags and suitcases piled near the front door. Evie slammed on her brakes.

Mum was holding a parcel, wrapped in pretty paper and tied with a bow. The label was in Grandma Iris' handwriting. Yes!

Wearing a huge grin, Evie took the parcel

into the front room to unwrap it in private –
away from her little sister Lily's curious eyes.
When she lifted the lid she saw a gorgeous
bracelet nestling snugly in tissue paper. It
was made of oblong beads that seemed to
zigzag their way around her wrist when she
slipped it on.

Evie turned the tissue paper over gently,
looking for a note from Grandma Iris. There
was usually one, with a clue to what sort of
magic the bracelet would do. There it was!
She lifted the card free and read,

In gear for a move, this time around,
Though you'll stay firmly on the ground,
I'll be in the air, as you'll discover.
Use the magic before it's over.

4

Hmm. Could it be to do with flying? Being in the air sounded like flying. On the other hand, it said pretty clearly that she'd be on the ground. Evie folded the wrapping paper away neatly. Her last gift had been a bracelet that let her fly. Would Grandma Iris send the same bracelet twice? They didn't look anything alike.

There was one good way to find out what the bracelet did – and that was to try it. Evie turned the bracelet on her wrist one, two, three times …

… golden light streamed out of it and twisted, dancing in the air. Magic! But what would it do? Evie looked around the room to see what had changed. Was she flying?

She looked down at her trainers. Nope.
Her feet were stuck firmly to the ground.
What else could the riddle mean? There
was something in the note about the sky.
Was that it? She looked at the windows.
Dad had already drawn the curtains closed,
so that nobody would be able to see they
weren't home while they were on holiday.
She couldn't see the sky through the heavy
fabric. Daft curtains – they needed to open.

She was about to walk over to the
window, when the strangest thing
happened. One of the curtains fluttered,
as though it was on a washing line. The
second one joined in, both flapping in a
non-existent breeze. Then, they pulled

themselves apart sharply and bright sunlight flooded into the room.

The curtains had moved by themselves.

No. The curtains had moved *because she wanted them to*. Her thoughts had made them move!

How brilliant was that?

She spun around the room looking to see what else she might move. Cushion float! she thought. The Keep Calm cushion that Mum loved wobbled on the settee. It tipped forward, like an overfull shopping bag, then righted itself smartly. It rose up, up, up until it bumped the ceiling. Evie laughed and the cushion plopped back down to earth.

'Evie?' Mum yelled. 'Are you nearly done packing? It's time to leave.'

'Yes!' Evie called back. This was going to be the best holiday ever.

They all squeezed into the people carrier: Mum and Dad, Lily and Evie, and her friends Isabelle and Ryan, plus all their bags and cases and bits for the journey. Evie had finally made everything squish into her case. Nana Em and Grandpa were making sure that Luna and Myla had their own holiday – the pets were staying round their house.

They were finally off! The city whizzed past. Rows of shops gave way to terraced houses, then the grey ribbon of the motorway. They sang 'There Were Ten in the Bed' and Lily yelled the loudest because she was the littlest. They played 'I spy' and, when they got tired, they all dozed for a while. They stopped for snacks at a service station where Dad grumbled at the cost. It seemed like hours and hours before the car rolled up a sandy drive into the caravan park.

'Woo-hoo!' Ryan shouted.

'I can see the sea!' Isabelle yelled.

'Pipe down, you lot,' Dad said. 'I'm going to find out which of the caravans are ours.'

Evie leaned forward, her head poking between the two front seats. 'Caravans?' she asked. 'What do you mean? Have we got more than one?' Usually they all squished into one and if it rained, everyone got on each other's nerves by the end of the week.

Mum flashed a funny glance at Dad. 'Never you mind,' she told Evie.

Evie grinned. Something was going on.

When Dad came back from the office, he took them to one of the big caravans with a view of the sandy bay below. The sea was blue and green like a postcard from Grandma Iris' home. Evie could make out families playing on the beach and a trail of donkeys giving rides. She leapt into the air

and raced three times around the caravan.
'Wheeeee!' she squealed.

'Happy?' Mum asked with a giggle.

'Happy,' Evie agreed. With her magic
bracelet, her friends and a week by the
seaside, this was going to be the best
holiday ever.

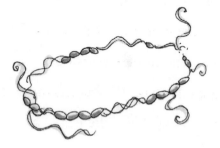

Chapter 2

Inside the static caravan, she and Isabelle had bunk beds, while Ryan had a blow-up mattress on the floor.

'I've got something to show you,' Evie said. She held up her wrist.

'A magic bracelet,' Isabelle said with delight.

'Hush. Mum always says the caravan walls are made of paper. They'll hear you,' Evie warned.

'A magic bracelet,' Isabelle whispered. 'What does it do?'

'Watch.'

She turned it three times and golden light streamed out into the small room. Evie thought hard, imagining what she wanted the objects to do. The pillows wobbled upright and pulled on their own pillow cases as though they were pulling on jumpers. The duvets flopped themselves flat on the bed. The small cupboard door slammed open and the coat hangers clicked off the railings and landed on their suitcases, ready for their clothes.

'Wow!' Ryan said. 'Telekinesis!'

'There's no telly in here,' Isabelle said.

'Telekinesis. It means moving things with your mind. Is that what you're doing, Evie?' he asked. He was smiling wide as the bay below the caravan.

She nodded. 'It's cool, isn't it?'

'Definitely,' he agreed.

They were interrupted by a knock on the door. 'Hey, you three, I'm headed to the Activity Centre. Do you want to find Kids' Club?' Dad said.

Woo-hoo!

She definitely did. There were always loads of great things to do at the Activity Centre.

They were unpacked in moments – with a little help from the bracelet – and they headed out with Dad. The centre was at the far end of the caravan park, where the grassy pitches turned sandy and dropped down into dunes. There, nestled in the spiky grass, was a metal warehouse. It was painted with blue waves crashing on the side and a bright yellow sun shining on the water. Evie ran towards it, with the others just behind. It was hard to run in sand, her feet sank and the ground shifted. She was out of breath by the time she reached the centre.

Dad strolled up last, grinning at them all. 'It's boating this afternoon,' he said, reading the chalkboard list that was propped up against an old wooden barrel. 'I'll sign you up.'

He went inside, leaving them to explore. The warehouse door was wide open and they could see wetsuits and life jackets, surfboards and sails all lined up neatly in racks. The sea rolled on to the beach with a gentle shush-shush-shush. On either side of the bay was the small village, and green headlands stretched out into the water, making a natural harbour.

'New landlubbers come to join my motley crew?' said a voice. It belonged to a young woman with dark hair and a cheeky smile who also had a brightly coloured parrot on her shoulder. 'Mind your cake hole!' the parrot squawked.

'Hello,' Evie said.

'I'm Captain Gwen,' the young woman said. 'And this is Silver, my parrot.'

'Golden Sands!' the parrot yelled.

'Don't mind Silver, he doesn't make much sense,' Gwen said. 'Right then, crew. Come and try on some life jackets and let's find you a rowboat. The shallows are roped off for boating, so you can't take her out too far. Let's get you shipshape!'

Dad waved from the beach as they splashed their way into the water. Their rowboat was bright red, with wooden oars. It was heavy to begin with, as it cut through the wet sand, but as soon as it hit the waves, it bobbed happily. Evie, Isabelle and Ryan kept pushing, until the water was up over their knees and they were all damp and salty. Isabelle climbed in first, scrambling to get out of the water. The others were right behind.

'Watch out!' Isabelle just missed Ryan as she spun the oars into place. Then they were off. Isabelle pulled and heaved, cutting through the water with the oars. It was hard work, but soon they skimmed over the bright blue water with seagulls swirling overhead.

The wind tugged at Evie's hair and the spray from the oars tasted of sun and sea. 'Woo-hoo!' she yelled again.

Isabelle, whose face was a bit red and puffed-out, handed the oars over to Ryan who took a turn. There were other boats out on the water, with other Kids' Club crews aboard – a yellow one, a blue one, a green one. They waved as they bobbed past.

'Careful!' a girl aboard the green boat yelled. 'You're headed straight for us!'

Ryan twisted in his seat and pulled his right oar sharply. 'Sorry! Just getting used to the steering.' They moved past the green boat with no damage.

'This is hard work,' Ryan complained.

'Why doesn't Evie help?' Isabelle suggested.

'I'll take a turn, of course I will,' Evie said.

'No,' Isabelle almost danced on her bench, 'I don't mean help with the oars. I meant

with your bracelet! Can you make the boat move by itself so none of us has to row?'

Evie felt herself tingle inside. Could she? The boat bobbed about all over the place, and it was bigger than anything she'd tried to move so far. But it was light in the water, so maybe she could? Then they could whizz over the water with no one struggling at the oars!

There was only one way to find out. Evie turned her bracelet, one, two, three times, and watched in delight as the gold light streamed out of it into the sunshine. She concentrated hard on the boat, urging it on through the waves. The prow cut through the water like a hot knife through butter.

The boat sped up, getting faster and faster, until it was skimming the waves. Wind whipped her hair about her face, they sped up until the beach was just a blur.

'Too fast!' Isabelle yelled. 'Watch out!' The little yellow rowboat seemed to appear from nowhere – right in front of them! Evie told the boat to turn, now, hard! The boat did, flipping to the right so fast that Evie lost her balance. The boat tilted, lurched. She tried to grip the sides, but it was no good. The whole boat flipped in the water – and all three fell in with a huge splash.

Chapter 3

Evie gasped as she dropped – plop – into the water.

'Eeek!' Isabelle yelled. 'It's freezing!'

Evie splashed about until her toes touched the bottom. Oh, they weren't out of their depth, she thought with relief. She stood up. The others did too. The waves splashed

around their waists. She was dripping wet.
Her clothes felt heavy and her hair stuck
to her face. The poor rowing boat bobbed
upside down beside them.

She heard the chug of a motor and turned
to see Gwen in a small boat powering
towards them. Silver the parrot hopped from
one leg to another on her shoulder. 'Man
overboard! Man overboard!' he squawked.

Gwen's boat pulled up alongside them,
sending little waves crashing into Evie's life
jacket. 'Are you all OK? What happened?'
Gwen asked anxiously.

Ryan wiped dripping water from his face.
'We just took a turn too fast, that's all.'

'I didn't even know that was possible. I've

never seen anything like that before!' Gwen
said. She leaned over the side of the boat
and grabbed Evie's arms. With a rush of
water, and a lot of splashing, Evie got into
the motorboat. She helped the others climb
aboard too. Gwen righted their wrecked
vessel, so that it bobbed the right way up
again. 'I'll tie it in, then take us back to
shore,' Gwen said. She tethered the little
red boat to hers, snaking the rope back and
forth quickly.

Ryan watched her do it. 'What sort of
knot is that?' he asked.

'A hitch knot. It's one of the things you'll
learn later this week. But first things first,
let's get you warm and dry!'

27

Gwen soon had them racing towards the beach and crunching on to the soft sand. There was no sign of Dad – he must have headed back to the caravan. But other people were staring as they dripped little puddles. The groups of families and children playing all turned to watch as they trooped back to the Activity Centre. Evie felt her cheeks blush. She shouldn't have tried to move something as big as a boat with magic, it was bound to go wrong. One man with a white beard and nut-brown wrinkly skin, as though it had seen all weathers more than once, glared at them. 'More idiots on the water, Gwen?' he growled.

'We all have to start somewhere, don't we,

Captain Dai?' Gwen replied cheerfully. 'In here,' she told Evie. 'Don't mind Dai. You're not the first crew to get a surprise dunking and you won't be the last. We've got a drying room at the back, you can sit in there until you don't squelch so much.'

The drying room was toasty. It was going to make Evie's hair frizzy as anything, but there was nothing she could do about that. There were wetsuits and life jackets arranged neatly on wooden shelves. Gwen gave them all towels and extra-large baggy T-shirts with the camp logo on them that came right down to their knees. Once they were in the oversized tops, with their hair wrapped in towels, Gwen said, 'You stay put until you've warmed right up, OK? Silver will be here to keep you company.'

The bright green and red parrot squawked and fluttered up on to a drying rack. Gwen left, and the three of them had a look around.

'Sorry,' Evie said quietly.

'What are you sorry for?' Isabelle asked. 'That was a proper adventure! We were faster than a speedboat out there, then Gwen did a daring rescue, and now we get to see a part of the centre that no one ordinary gets to see.'

Evie smiled at her friend. There was no one who could match Isabelle for seeing the bright side of things.

Ryan didn't look too bothered either. He was exploring the room, the posters on the walls about tide times and sailing knots, the laminated maps with sea currents marked, the sections of rope coiled tidily, he even stopped in front of Silver for a closer look.

'Mind your beak!' the parrot said, when Ryan got too close.

'Sorry!' Ryan stepped back.

'It's almost as if he knows what he's saying,' Isabelle laughed.

Ryan's head tilted to one side. He knew a lot about animals, but had never seen a real parrot before today. 'I don't think they do know,' he said. 'I think they just repeat things they've heard before. It's more like he's playing back recordings than speaking for real.'

The parrot raised one of its clawed feet and shuffled across the shelf. Its feathers ruffled, as though it were cross with the world in general and Ryan in particular.

32

'So.' Isabelle stood beside Ryan. 'You're saying when the parrot talks, we're overhearing conversations he's heard in the past?'

'I guess so.'

'Cool,' Isabelle said. 'I wonder if he ever lived with pirates. Did you, Silver? Were you ever on a pirate ship?'

'Golden Sands,' Silver said excitedly. 'Golden Sands! Golden Sands!' He hopped up and down on his perch, his head nodding and bobbing as if he were at the campsite Friday disco.

Isabelle's eyes saucered wide. 'He was on a pirate ship! It must have been called the *Golden Sands*. Silver sailed the seven seas

33

and made scurvy dogs walk the plank.'

'Golden Sands! Golden Sands!' Silver
shrieked.

Evie wrung the last drops of water from
her hair and wiped the towel across the
back of her neck. She could feel the seawater
steaming off her in the heat.

'Golden Sands!' the bird cried, bobbing merrily away.

'Did you ever see any pirate treasure?' Isabelle asked him.

Silver went silent.

'He can't say because pirates never reveal their secrets,' Isabelle said.

'No,' Ryan replied. 'He can't say because he's just a parrot and he doesn't know any secrets.'

'Pieces of eight,' Silver said, very softly. 'Pieces of eight.'

'What's "pieces of eight"?' Isabelle asked.

Evie had no idea. She shrugged.

Ryan groaned. 'It's a kind of silver coin.'

'Really?' Isabelle practically squealed.

'I saw it in a film once,' Ryan said.

Evie could tell exactly what Isabelle was thinking – she was inventing stories about the Treasure of the *Golden Sands*.

'Where is it, Silver? What happened to the treasure?' Isabelle asked.

The parrot swivelled his head one way, then the other, as though he were spying for enemies.

Evie didn't think he was going to speak again. She picked up her shorts – they were damp, but not too bad. She pulled them on. Her trainers were still super squelchy. She'd seen enough of the sea today, if she was being honest.

'Silver, tell us, you *have* to tell us,' Isabelle

tried again. 'Where's the Treasure of the *Golden Sands*?'

Silver ducked his head so that it was close to his feet. 'Salty scraps. Mind your cake hole,' was all he said.

Chapter 4

'Salty scraps?' Isabelle repeated. She put her hands on her hips and looked put out. 'Is that a clue? Silver, that doesn't make any sense.'

The parrot hopped up and down on the drying rack. He stretched his feathers and clicked his beak. 'Salty scraps. Pieces of eight!' Silver clicked once more then tucked his head into his wing. He had clearly had enough of sharing his secrets.

Evie hung her towel up to dry. 'Maybe he doesn't know where the treasure is?' she suggested.

Isabelle swung around. 'Don't give up yet. He can't come right out and tell us, can he? I mean if he told every Tom, Dick and Harriet his secret, the treasure would have been found yonks ago.'

Ryan was still gazing at the posters on the walls. He was really getting into the life of a sailor! He peered closely at the green and blue contours of the coastline.

'Ryan!' Isabelle snapped. 'Pay attention.

What could "salty scraps" be a clue to? A scrap means a fight, doesn't it? Perhaps there was a fight near the sea?'

Ryan nodded slowly. Evie couldn't tell if he was being serious or just playing Isabelle's game. 'I hate to say it, but I think Isabelle might be right. I've found something.' He pointed to the map on the wall.

Evie and Isabelle both rushed over to see. Ryan's fingertip pointed to a bay, where the sea scooped into the headland. The bay was labelled in old-fashioned, swirly writing – Salty Cove.

'It's a place!' Isabelle gasped. 'Salty Cove is a place. Perhaps Silver saw a fight there between enemy pirates and that was the Salty Scrap! Ryan, you're brilliant.'

It wasn't often that Isabelle complimented Ryan, so he looked very pleased with himself.

'Where is the cove?' Evie asked. She knew a little bit about reading maps, because Dad sometimes let her navigate using the map on his phone – but the map on the wall didn't

have a handy blue dot to tell her where
she was.

Ryan moved his finger as he spoke.
'There's the campsite here, see? And this
is the big bay that we're on now. Salty
Cove is just north, on the other side of the
headland.'

It wasn't far. Maybe ten minutes' walk.
But Evie wasn't sure about this new
adventure. They'd already fallen in the
water! She didn't want Mum and Dad
to worry. Isabelle must have noticed her
dithering. 'I left my phone in my backpack
outside,' Isabelle said. 'We can ring
your mum and ask for permission to go
exploring.'

That was different. As long as Mum was OK, then Evie was more than happy to go looking for buried treasure – it was what holidays were made for, after all!

'Let's do it,' Evie said.

Evie called Mum, who didn't mind them exploring the headland and the beach as long as they stayed together and didn't go into the water – again. 'Have a lovely adventure. Make sure you're back for tea,' Mum said. 'There's a surprise for you later.'

That sounded exciting, but Mum wouldn't say any more, no matter how much Evie begged.

Isabelle and Ryan were more or less dry, so, as soon as Evie finished talking to Mum, they went to search for Salty Cove. Silver stayed at the Activity Centre with Gwen.

The path to the cove ran between the shore and the small row of shops that sold brightly coloured buckets and spades, fishing nets, body boards and anything else anyone might need beside the sea.

'Wait a sec,' Isabelle said. She ducked into one of the shops and came out holding a red spade with a wooden handle. 'We're going to need this for digging!' she explained.

The sandy path wound up between prickly gorse bushes and spiky marram grasses. The headland was like a finger poking out into the sea. There were a few people on the headland, walking their dogs, and flying kites. A breeze glided in from the sea, bringing the taste of salt and seaweed.

'Which way to the cove?' Evie asked.

'We shouldn't follow the main path,' Ryan said. 'That just leads straight out along the headland to admire the view from the end. We need to look for the way down on the other side.'

The path narrowed, so that they had to walk one behind the other. It dropped down and Evie could see the golden sand of the hidden cove nestled into the rocky land below. But where was the way down?

The path curled back towards the town and the main beach. There was no path at all that led down into Salty Cove!

'Well,' Ryan said, 'if there's no way to get to it, then it's a perfect place to hide pirate treasure.'

'Evie,' Isabelle said, 'could you use magic, do you think? You could lower us gently down to the beach?'

Evie pressed her lips together tightly. It was the word 'gently' that made her wince. She hadn't managed to be at all gentle when she'd powered the boat earlier. The idea of accidentally dropping her friends was too horrible. 'I don't know if I can,' she said.

It was at that moment that Ryan turned around. He'd heard a noise. Someone walking in their direction.

The man who crunched his way across

47

marram grass towards them was grumpy-looking. He frowned under his grey-white beard and tugged down his navy fishing cap to shield his eyes from the sun. His eyes crinkled in annoyance under his bushy eyebrows. Evie recognised him as the man who'd been mean earlier – Captain Dai. 'What are you lot up to?' he growled.

'We're looking for Salty Cove,' Isabelle said cheerfully. 'Do you know how to get there?'

Captain Dai nodded slowly. 'Yeah. Some silly fools have tied a rope above it, just at the cliff's edge, to climb up and down. Daft idea. It isn't somewhere anyone should go.'

'Why not?' Ryan asked.

'No respect for nature, some people. Thinking they can do whatever they want.'

He was the grumpiest person Evie had met in a long time. But he'd told them what to look out for. Her eyes scanned the ground, following the curve of the headland. There! Partly hidden by bushes, she could see a post, with a rope tied around it. The rope ran down, over the edge. A shallow ditch had been worn into the sandy soil by people climbing up and down.

'You stay away from there, you hear? The sands might be golden, but they're trouble,' Captain Dai growled at them.

Evie jumped, alarmed by the gruffness in the man's voice. What was down on Salty Cove that he didn't want them to see?

Chapter 5

Isabelle bounced up and down on her toes, waiting impatiently for the captain to carry on his walk along the headland.

'Pirate,' she hissed, as soon as he was out of sight. 'Did you see the size of his beard? Pirate, for sure. I think he was one of the ones that buried the treasure in the first place. Did you hear what he said about the beach? He said it had *Golden Sands*. That's the name of the ship Silver talked about! *And* he was hanging around the boathouse – he must have been looking for a chance to kidnap Silver back from Gwen!'

Evie didn't want to point out that Silver hadn't mentioned a ship at all – this was all getting too exciting. Was Isabelle's story right? Could the man really be a pirate, trying to scare them away from his silver coins?

'He didn't scare me,' Evie said, ignoring her slightly jelly knees.

'Me neither,' Isabelle agreed. 'Come on.'

The drop down to the beach was not like

any path Evie had seen before. It was too steep to walk down, but the rope was there as a kind of banister. If she held on tight, she'd be able to half-walk, half-drop down. It was about the height of the top diving board at the swimming pool. At the bottom was a beautiful beach, like something from a postcard, with no one else on it at all.

'I'll go first,' Isabelle said. She gripped the rope tightly and stepped over the edge. Ryan was right behind, then it was Evie's turn. She took it slowly and carefully, feeling for each foothold with the tip of her still damp trainers.

'Hey!'

She was about halfway down when she

53

heard the shout coming from above. She looked up. The grumpy man was back! His face looked more red than brown – he was angry! He shook his fist and yelled something that she couldn't make out. The wind whipped his words away.

He must be trying to protect his treasure!

Evie quickened her pace, trying not to let the rope burn as it ran through her hands. The angry shouts were getting louder and the man got more and more cross.

She thumped down on to the sliding sand. Above her, the man's legs swung out over the edge of the headland – he was going to follow them down!

Thinking quickly, Evie reached for her

bracelet. She turned it one, two, three times and as soon as the snaking gold magic slipped out of it and up her arm, she stared hard at the rope – move, move, move, she thought, over and over.

The rope listened.

It slithered and twitched.

The man holding the rope felt it move. She heard him grunt in alarm, then he scrambled back up to the top to get away from the wriggling rope.

Evie waited until his feet disappeared up over the edge. Then, she thought hard about the knot that kept the rope in place. In her mind, she saw the end loosen. She urged it to untie itself. A moment later, the rope slithered all the way down to land with a thump on the beach.

She'd done it! She'd stopped him following them down!

'Oh-oh,' Ryan said.

Evie felt her victorious grin fade. 'What?'

'How are we going to get back up now?' Ryan asked.

Evie looked at the steep slope – the climb was too difficult without the rope.

'She can just tie it up again with magic,' Isabelle said breezily, 'or we can just walk around the headland back to the main beach.'

Evie sighed with relief. Isabelle was right. She could see that although they were in a

cove, the white sand stretched out all the
way around the rocks of the headland. They
would be able to follow the edge of the cliff
around to the main beach. The roped path
was just a shortcut.

She took in the wide cove, twirling
in an eager circle. They were the only
people there. They had a whole beach to
themselves! The cliffs rose high above.
They were formed of layers of rocks,
tipped up on their sides like books on a
bookshelf – grey, blue and black stripes
with one or two small trees doing their
best to grow out of them. The sea rolled
in gentle waves, leaving green and brown
seaweed behind. Above she could hear

the shriek of seagulls and the whole place
smelled of salt and summer.

'Where's the treasure buried?' Isabelle
asked. She propped her spade on her
shoulder and held her free hand up to
shade her eyes.

'Without a map, we'll just have to dig

random holes and hope for the best,' Ryan said glumly.

They hadn't really thought about this part of the quest, Evie realised.

'Did Silver give us any more clues?' Isabelle asked. 'What else did he say?'

'Just nonsense about pieces of eight and cake holes,' Evie said, feeling as glum as Ryan had sounded.

Isabelle wasn't put off at all. She strode across the beach as if she were a conquering pirate looking for a safe place for her loot.

'You just have to think like a pirate,' she said. 'Argh, my land-lubbing cronies, where be a good place for my coins on this here beach?'

Evie had to giggle. Isabelle sounded like something from a film. 'Aye, aye, Cap'n,' she replied. 'We'll set a course for safe harbour and find a fine place for treasure.'

Evie whooped and raced across the beach. In her imagination their galleon was anchored in the bay, its white sails billowing and the Jolly Roger flying atop the mast. The pirate crew on board had trusted them to find a perfect hiding spot for the treasure.

It didn't matter whether the treasure was real, she realised, it was just great to have an adventure looking for it. She hollered in delight, kicking sand up in the air and leaping the piles of driftwood and seaweed. She was a pirate for a day! Ryan was right behind her, waving his imaginary cutlass and bellowing at the top of his lungs.

Then, Isabelle slammed on the brakes. Evie could almost see her quiver with excitement before she turned and yelled, 'Guys, come and take a look at this!'

Chapter 6

Isabelle was at the top of the beach, set back from the sea. She had pushed her spade into the sand and was waving both arms above her head. 'Guys, come and look!'

Evie and Ryan didn't need to be invited twice. They raced each other to reach her. Ryan was taller, but Evie had a better stride.

They were neck and neck and both tumbled down on to the sand beside Isabelle at the exact same moment.

'What is it?' Evie said between gasps.

'That!' Isabelle pointed at the spot where the cliff met the sand. There were big boulders, rocks that had fallen free, and rock pools glistened brightly in the sunshine. But it wasn't the crabs and starfish that Isabelle was excited by. Nestled in the shadows of the boulders was a cave.

The opening was narrow, but tall. An adult would have to walk in sideways, but it was just the right size for Evie.

She shivered, despite the sunshine. There was something scary about the dark, damp

cave mouth, it looked like a secret the cliff was keeping.

'What do you think?' Isabelle whispered above the hissing of the sea.

'If I were a pirate, that's where I'd bury my treasure,' Ryan said.

'That's what I thought,' Isabelle replied.

They were both looking at her. Waiting to see if she agreed.

Should they go in? It looked scary, and everyone knew that monsters lived in caves. But then, monsters weren't real, so … She rocked back and forth on her feet, feeling the sand crunch as she thought.

Then, she took a deep breath. 'Let's do it,' she said.

Isabelle fumbled for her phone and
switched on the torch. The beam was weak,
but it was better than nothing. By its light,
Evie could see the slippery, black walls of
the cave. Isabelle went in first, then Evie,
with Ryan last.

67

The walls were closer than Evie liked. She held her palms out and felt the wetness of them as she inched forward. Isabelle blocked out a lot of the light and Evie found herself stumbling over small stones and rocks. Something dripped on to her neck and she squished down a yelp. The air was much colder in here than it was outside and the smell of rotting seaweed was strong.

But soon, the walls spread and there was more room to stand upright. The entrance had just been a narrow tunnel into the proper cave.

Evie gasped. The space they found themselves in was amazing. The cave opened right out and a dome of rock above their heads dripped with pale stalactites, like huge icicles. Stalagmites stretched up from the floor to meet them. Isabelle swung her torch beam around. The space was so big the light couldn't reach far enough to show the edges of the cave.

'We shouldn't go too far,' Ryan warned. 'There might be branching tunnels and it would be easy to get lost.'

Isabelle nodded. 'I think you're right. And the pirates on board the Golden Sands would have thought so too. So, I think this is the perfect spot to dig. Here.' She passed Ryan her phone. 'Shine the light on the ground.'

Ryan held the phone while Isabelle crunched her spade into the damp sand.

Evie pulled away any loose stones to make
the digging easier. In no time at all, Isabelle
had cleared enough sand to make a hole
big enough to sit in. With every cut that the
spade made, Evie listened out for the sound
of plastic on wood – the sound of a spade
hitting a treasure chest. Her chest fizzed
with excitement and bursts of gold magic
shimmered around the cave wall.

But there was no noise.

No sign of the treasure chest.

Then, something puzzling happened.
The hole, growing bigger by the minute,
began to fill with water. Evie could see the
reflection from the torch glittering on the
surface of the new pool. Isabelle had to stop
digging, because the spade splashed down
into shifting sand.

'Where's the water coming from?' Isabelle
asked. 'We've dug a well!'

Evie noticed the torch shaking in Ryan's
hand. 'It's seawater,' he said. He glanced
back over his shoulder, and shone the
torch into the tunnel. Evie saw more water
reflecting light back at them.

'It's seawater,' Ryan gasped. 'The tide's coming in!'

Evie realised the danger in an instant. The seawater was rising in the hole, and they were caught at the wrong end of a narrow tunnel. 'We have to get out, now!' she said.

The others leapt into action. Ryan led the way, still holding Isabelle's phone. Then Isabelle, with Evie at the back. It was hard to see where she was going; her hands caught on the jaggy rocks, grazing her palms. The light went out completely as Ryan stumbled and fell. Isabelle helped him up. They all groped their way along in darkness. She could feel water seeping into her trainers. The ground squelched as she ran.

Then, they could see daylight. The welcome yellow and blue of the beach and sky. They tumbled out in relief. Evie had never felt so pleased to feel sunshine on her skin.

The sea was much nearer the cliffs than it was when they'd gone in. The tide was definitely moving in.

'That was a close call,' Ryan said. 'I'm sorry, Isabelle, but your phone didn't make it.' He held up her phone; its screen was cracked. 'It broke when I fell.'

Isabelle looked cross for a second, then shrugged. 'It's OK, it was an accident. I can get it mended. Well, Mum can.'

'We should get out of here,' Evie said.

73

The tide turning in the tunnel had been a bit too scary for her taste. It would be nice to get back to the caravan and change into some dry shoes.

She headed away from the cave entrance, towards the sliver of sand that ran around the headland back to the main beach. And saw that it was barely there at all – it was being drowned by the rising tide.

Chapter 7

'Run!' Evie yelled.

The waves were rolling up over the beach, covering the pathway that led to the main beach, and safety.

Isabelle dropped her spade. It was clear that they had to sprint if they were to have any chance of making it before the tide covered the path completely. Evie powered forwards. She clenched the muscles in her arms, pulling them back and forth through the air. Her legs pounded into the sand, pushing her nearer and nearer the path. Her friends were right beside her, running hard. Faster. Faster. They had to get there. Time seemed to slow. She could see the glisten of every wave, rolling further and further up the shore.

Fifty metres to go.

Thirty metres.

Ten metres.

They might just make it.

She slammed on the brakes as a wave, bigger than any so far, crashed over the

path. It didn't roll back out. The path was underwater.

'Could we wade across?' Isabelle wondered aloud.

Evie had a stitch in her side, and could barely talk, but she shook her head firmly. 'Too dangerous,' she managed to say.

Ryan had both hands on his head and

stared out to sea. 'How long, do you think, before the tide comes into the cove completely?'

The sea seemed to be creeping up the beach so quickly, it was hard to know. To Evie, every time she blinked the sea was a little bit closer.

'Can we climb the rope path?' Isabelle's voice trembled with the same fear that Evie was feeling. They were trapped on the beach with the waves getting rougher and closer by the second!

'Call the coastguard,' Evie suggested, 'or Mum. They both rescue people.'

'Phone's dead,' Isabelle said.

Ryan hung his head in shame.

'It doesn't matter,' Evie said quickly. 'We'll come up with another plan.' She ran back up the beach to the point where the rope path met the sand. The blue rope was still coiled at her feet, where it had fallen. The narrow path was worn smooth, and was as slippery as a ski slope. Evie jumped up and tried to climb, but her hands slid over the packed red clay.

There was no way they were going to be able to climb out of the bay. Safety was twenty metres straight up, and they couldn't reach it.

'Your bracelet!' Isabelle cried. 'You can move us all with magic!'

Evie felt as though the panic was washed away with that one sentence. Of course! She could whisk them all up to the top just by thinking about it. She could have hugged Isabelle for making the suggestion, but there was no time to lose.

She turned her bracelet, once, twice, three times … gold light appeared and she thought, as hard as she possibly could, that Isabelle should fly up to safety.

Nothing happened.

'What's wrong?' Ryan asked.

'I don't know!' Evie whispered. She tried again. Willing Isabelle to float up to the top of the cliff with everything she had. Up, up, up, she thought.

Isabelle raised an eyebrow. 'Is it working? Am I moving?'

'No,' Evie whispered, 'it isn't working.' Was she not trying hard enough? Was she getting it wrong somehow?

Isabelle jumped up and down, trying to help the magic along. 'I don't get it. You moved the rope and the boat and all our packing. You've gotten really good at magic.'

Evie glanced at the sea and the waves rolling closer and closer. She wasn't good when it mattered. She felt tears pricking her eyes.

Isabelle's feet stayed firmly on the ground.

'It hasn't been three days, has it?' Ryan asked. Evie shook her head – they had got into trouble before because the magic only lasted three days. But it had only been half a

81

day since she opened Grandma Iris' gift.

Then, with a flash, Evie remembered Grandma Iris' note. It had said,

"In gear for a move, this time around,

Though you'll stay firmly on the ground".

It was *gear* – stuff, things, objects – that could move, not people. She'd be staying on the ground. It wasn't flying magic in the bracelet and Grandma Iris had told her so in the riddle.

Her plan wasn't going to work.

She felt Ryan's hand on her shoulder. 'Don't worry,' he said. 'We'll think of something. We've been in worse situations than this before.'

The sound of waves sucking at the sand,

rolling shining, clattering pebbles, was louder now. Ryan had to shout for Evie to hear him.

'How about the rope?' Isabelle bellowed. 'Can you retie it at the top?'

Evie reached for her bracelet and sent magic whipping up around the rope. It hovered, and rose, like a snake uncoiling. Golden light swirled around it as it swayed upwards. It was going to work! She could do it!

Just then a wave washed right over her trainers. She felt the cold salty water soak through the fabric. As it rushed back out to sea the wave made her wobble and clutch Ryan to stop from falling. But she didn't stop looking at the rope. It was near the top of the path now, headed back to the stake it had been tied to. She just had to think of it forming a knot, wrapping around the wood and twisting and looping in tight.

Another wave crashed into her legs, up to her knees this time. It knocked her forwards. Water splashed up her arms, soaking her clothes.

It broke her concentration.

The rope slithered back down and

splashed into the water.

'Come on, Evie,' Ryan insisted. 'The tide's too close.'

'I can tie the rope! I know I can. I just need another try.'

'There's no time. We have to get out of the water.'

Evie struggled to her feet. The water was swirling around her calves. The next wave rolled in even higher.

Ryan was right.

They were out of time.

Chapter 8

Evie, Isabelle and Ryan were pushed back up the beach by the advancing sea. The tide was coming in fast. They stumbled backwards. Isabelle slipped on some seaweed. Evie tripped over a piece of driftwood and only just stopped herself from splashing back into the water.

Soon they were back by the cave mouth, with nowhere else to go.

'Can we climb, do you reckon?' Isabelle asked. She reached up and grabbed at the overhanging rock. But she couldn't find a handhold and she fell straight back down.

'We should try yelling,' Ryan suggested. 'Help! Help!'

They all shouted as loudly as they could. But the wind and the sound of the sea swept their voices away. Though Evie kept her eyes up, watching the cliff top, no friendly face appeared.

They were on their own.

A wave surged forward and a thick piece of driftwood, almost a tree trunk, rolled with it.

As she watched it settle back into the sand, Evie had an idea. 'The wood!' she yelped. 'We can get all the pieces of driftwood and turn them into a raft. Then, I can use the magic to steer us back to the main beach.'

Isabelle looked at the tideline and nodded eagerly. 'Worth a try.'

'I think it could work,' Ryan agreed. They both sounded scared, but they stood straight with their heads high, trying not to let her see how worried they were. Evie had just enough time to remember, for the hundredth time, how amazing her friends were, before she leapt into action.

There was a fringe of flotsam and jetsam

89

along the high tidemark – seaweed and mermaid's purses, lengths of rope and twine, bottles and buzzing flies, all tangled up together. And dotted through it all, Evie could see dozens of lengths of wood. They were all shapes and sizes, some as thick as lamp-posts, others more like her arm. There were enough to make the raft. If they worked fast enough.

Evie reached for her bracelet and turned it, once, twice, three times …

… and as soon as the golden light streamed out, she imagined every single piece of wood on the beach floating up in the air and heading straight towards them.

The effect was instant.

All around brown, bleached, grey and
black pieces of wood shrugged off the sand
and seaweed and jolted up into the air. They
hovered above the ground before whizzing
to make a pile at Evie's feet.

The stack was bigger than the bonfire at
Halloween! It was definitely enough to make
a raft.

'Now for the rope!' Evie said in delight.

She thought hard, and the beach seemed
to shimmer as the strands of rope pulled
themselves from the tideline. Red, orange,
blue, they shot up like streamers from party
poppers. The rope strands danced across
the sand and fluttered in a pile beside the
wood. Even the long section that had helped

them down to the beach curled up like a puppy at her feet.

'We just have to tie them all together,' she said.

'Can't magic do that?' Isabelle asked.

Evie frowned, her eyebrows drawn close together. 'I don't think so. I have to imagine what it is I want the object to do, and then it does it. But I only know how to do one knot. The one I use on my trainers. That isn't strong enough to hold a raft together, is it?'

'I can do it!' Ryan said in excitement. He dropped down on to his knees and tugged two big bits of wood free from the pile. He grabbed a length of bright orange rope. 'There was a poster about knots in the

93

Activity Centre. I remember them. We need to use a square lash.'

Ryan grabbed both ends of a piece of rope. He glanced at the incoming sea. Evie saw that his hands were shaking. He dropped one end of the rope.

'It's OK,' she told him. 'Take a deep breath. You can do it. Don't think about why you're doing this. Just imagine we're all just here on the beach, playing. And you're showing us a cool thing you've learned. How's that?'

Ryan nodded. He closed his eyes for a second and forced his breathing to slow. Then, his eyes opened and he started again with the knot.

94

'It's simple really,' he said. 'This end goes there, around there, through there, and ...'

Ryan crossed the wood to make a corner, then whipped the orange rope around the join, weaving it in and out.

'... done!'

The two bits of wood were firmly held together.

Evie felt herself grinning. This was going to work!

She and Isabelle helped with the next knot. Then they all three worked as fast as they could, lashing the wood pile together until they had a rough platform that was big enough for them all to sit on.

They were just in time.

As Evie tied the last knot a wave washed over her feet, right up to her ankles.

'Yuck!' Isabelle shrieked. 'My shoes are soaking again.'

'Don't worry about that now,' Evie said. 'Jump aboard, let's see if our raft actually floats.'

They all scrambled on to their makeshift

vessel. The wood sank into the wet sand with their weight. Before too long, the sea rolled in, lapping up against the cliff and running into the cave mouth.

The cove was completely under water.

But on board their raft, the three found themselves rocking up and down, floating. Water slid between the raft poles, but the knots all held. The raft was at sea!

'Whoa, careful.'

'Watch out.'

'Oops.'

They all jostled for space on the moving raft. One wave lifted them right up, before pulling them away from the land and out towards open water. Salt spray sparkled in the air, Evie could taste it on her lips.

They really were at sea!

Then, she realised with a leap of alarm that they really *were* at sea. The waves had pushed them right out of the cove and they were caught in a strong current. The wind was whipping through her hair. They had picked up speed. The cliffs were in the distance now and the deep water below was dark and cold.

Evie knew that if they were swept out to sea, this raft would be just as dangerous as staying in the cove. It was time to use more magic!

Chapter 9

Evie turned the bracelet on her wrist, once, twice, three times. The gold light that shot out sparkled like sunlight on the crests of the waves.

Head to shore, she thought hard. Head to shore!

The raft responded immediately. It

skimmed over the water like a magic carpet, picking up speed. As it dashed across the bay, it sliced the top off waves, sending dancing rainbows up into the sky.

'Woo-hoo!' Isabelle cried. 'This is fun.'

'Hold on tight,' Evie warned. The raft was harder to steer than the boat earlier – and she had managed to capsize that.

They were rounding the headland. The rocks rose up above them on the left-hand side of the raft; the wide, open sea stretched out to their right.

As they cleared the tip of the headland, Evie realised, with a horrified gasp, that there was something in their way.

Their path was blocked by a fishing boat.

They were headed straight for it.

Evie had to take evasive action!

Stop! Stop! Stop! she thought as hard as she could at the raft. It responded. The wooden poles, lashed together, rippled and clattered as they pulled back. The knots creaked. The raft bucked like an angry horse. Seawater splashed over them all, splattering her nose and mouth. Evie gasped, but clung to the raft so tightly her knuckles turned pale.

The raft skidded, twisted, strained … and then slowed. The energy drained out of it and it floated, gently, until it bumped against the hull of the boat.

Evie sighed. They were all still in one piece, and so was their raft.

103

She had enough time to take in the neat blue paintwork of the hull and the bright orange nets that dangled over the edge, when she heard an angry yell from above.

'You lot!' the voice said.

She looked up to see Captain Dai, looking more cross than she had ever seen him before.

'Shiver my timbers,' Isabelle said, 'we're about to be scuppered.'

'Maybe we're about to be rescued,' Ryan replied. 'Ahoy!' he yelled up.

The captain growled. Then disappeared for a second, before returning with a bright orange lifebuoy. He threw the ring over the side and it landed with a splash beside their raft. The buoy was connected to the boat by a white rope.

'Climb up,' he instructed.

One by one, Evie, Ryan and Isabelle climbed from the raft into the safety of the fishing boat. They were all soaking wet. Evie's legs felt a bit wobbly from the climb, so she sank down on to the deck gratefully.

It felt good and solid against her back. In spite of the smell of fish and engine oil, she was very, very glad to be there.

'I told you lot not to go to Sandy Cove,' Captain Dai said. 'Any fool could see the tide was turning. It was only a matter of time until the whole beach was a playground for the fish.'

He'd been trying to warn them about the tide? Evie felt herself blush. They'd been wrong not to listen to him, even if he did seem like the Grumpiest Man in Grumptown.

Isabelle and Ryan huddled down on the deck of the boat beside her and they bobbed gently on the waves.

Captain Dai grinned suddenly, and surprisingly! 'I like that little raft you made, though. Someone's handy with their sea skills.'

'That was Ryan,' Isabelle said. 'He learned some knots.'

'I'd say he did. Maybe Gwen will teach you something after all. This is my little boat, the *Rhiannon*. Welcome aboard.'

Captain Dai ducked into the small cabin and came back a few minutes later with an armful of old towels and a big bar of chocolate. 'You'll be needing these, I suppose,' he said.

Once they'd dried themselves off – for the second time that day – and eaten chocolate,

Evie felt like she had her sea legs back. She hung the towels on a handrail to dry. The *Rhiannon* was travelling across the bay. Evie shielded her eyes from the glare of the sun and looked at the stretch of golden beach and the colourful figures playing in the sand.

'We were looking for the Treasure of the *Golden Sands*,' she told the captain.

'Hush!' Isabelle snapped. 'We don't know for sure he's not a pirate.'

Captain Dai half-smiled. 'It's true. You don't know that for sure. In fact, I do have an interest in the treasure of the Golden Sands myself.'

'You do?' Isabelle's eyes were practically on stalks.

'I do,' he replied, very seriously. 'I can take you there myself, if you'd like?'

Evie caught Ryan's eye. It would be lovely to carry on the search, to hunt for treasure and play at pirate games. But Mum and Dad would be getting worried, and they'd almost been swept out to sea already.

Ryan shook his head. 'Thanks, but we

should probably stop playing now.'

'We weren't playing!' Isabelle insisted. 'Silver the parrot knows what he's talking about.'

'That he does. He's not as bird-brained as some,' Captain Dai agreed. He was standing near a steering wheel and he made a few gentle corrections to their course, nudging the *Rhiannon* towards land. 'But it just so happens that when we come in to land, we go right past the Golden Sands. So, it's on our way, if you want to see it?'

The *Golden Sands* was real? Evie could hardly believe it. She'd thought all this time that they were just playing make-believe. But the pirate ship was real? Her mouth flew

110

open and her eyebrows were raised like the Jolly Roger.

Captain Dai saw and his half-smile became a chuckle. 'I'll take that as a yes.' He turned the wheel again and Evie felt the boat tip, ever so gently, as she turned. He was a much better sailor than she was!

The *Rhiannon* was headed to a wooden jetty, at the village end of the beach. It stuck out into the sea and there were lots of small boats and dinghies moored beside it.

'I can tie a hitch knot!' Ryan said as the boat nudged gently against the wooden piles of the jetty.

'Tie her off then,' Captain Dai said. Which Evie assumed meant 'make sure the boat doesn't float away once we get out', because Ryan leapt into action. He tied the tethering rope securely and they all clambered up a ladder that Captain Dai hooked in place.

There, at the top of the steps, was the Golden Sands.

Chapter 10

'I'll leave you here, then,' the captain said gruffly. 'You know where you are?'

Evie did. They were on the harbour jetty, in front of a small row of shops: an arcade, the souvenir shop, and the fish and chip restaurant. The Golden Sands.

'It's a takeaway?' Isabelle asked in disgust.

Evie felt laughter bubbling up inside.

'Not just a takeaway,' Captain Dai said. 'This is the best fish and chip restaurant on the whole west coast. I should know. I sell them my fish.' He chuckled as he climbed back down to the *Rhiannon* and set sail again.

Evie, Isabelle and Ryan stood in front of the restaurant. It was a stone building, with grey roof tiles and window boxes full of bright red geraniums. Over the door there was a sign showing a fish in a chef's hat.

Evie began to laugh. And soon the other two joined in. They might be soggy, and drippy, and a little bit cold, but they had had a proper adventure – and all because a parrot liked chips!

'Salty scraps!' Isabelle gasped. 'Of course. Silver was talking about the tasty bits at the bottom of your chips.'

The giggles bubbled over again.

'Evie!' She heard Mum's voice, coming from the restaurant door. 'There you are! I was wondering if you got my text. Why are you all wet? You didn't go swimming, did you?' Mum bustled out, her eyes crinkled with concern.

'Not exactly,' Evie said.

'Well, I'm glad you made it in time. Come in, come in.'

What was going on? Why was Mum in the Golden Sands? Evie exchanged looks

115

with Isabelle. But Isabelle made a 'not-a-clue' face.

They followed Mum inside.

The restaurant smelled of sea and salt and frying. It made Evie's tummy rumble. Fish weren't just on the menu, there were paintings of fish on the walls, and fishing nets decorating the alcoves. Even the salt and pepper shakers on the tables were in the shape of fish. There were a few groups of people sitting with ginormous plates of battered cod and mushy peas and thick-cut chips.

Then she realised that she recognised the people at one of the tables – Dad and Mum, Lily, and –

Her breath caught in her throat.

Grandma Iris.

It was really her. Sitting at the table as if it were the most normal thing in the world. Grandma Iris was here.

Evie stumbled across the restaurant. She barely noticed the chairs she bumped into. She didn't care about the tears on her cheeks. She just wanted to get to Grandma.

Grandma Iris had tears in her eyes too and Evie tumbled into her outstretched arms. She felt Grandma's hands on her back, pulling her into a tight snuggle. Grandma smelled of perfume and skin cream and love.

'You're here, you're really here,' Evie whispered.

117

'As if by magic!' Grandma Iris whispered
back.

Evie felt the giggles surge. And the tears.
She had no idea if she was laughing or
crying as Mum pulled out a chair for her.

'Here, you and Lily can sit either side of

Grandma. Ryan, Isabelle, in you get, there's room for everyone.'

Evie sat down, but she didn't want to stop touching Grandma Iris – she couldn't believe she was real! – so she kept a hold of her hand across the table.

'You didn't guess I was coming?' Grandma Iris asked.

Evie shook her head. 'Not at all.'

'We kept it a surprise, Mama,' Dad said. He looked delighted with himself. Evie wondered if he'd looked that way when he was a little boy and saw his mum every day.

'We hired an extra caravan for you,' Mum added. 'But we kept it a surprise.'

'It's a lovely surprise!' Lily said.

119

It was. Evie's fingers crept towards the bracelet at her wrist. Grandma Iris, who was still holding Evie's hand, noticed and gave her a little squeeze.

Mum handed out menus. 'We're going to have a slap-up tea to celebrate everyone being together. Anything you like. Push the boat out.'

'Unless you three have had enough of boats for one day?' Dad asked.

Evie rolled her eyes, but read the menu. Once they'd ordered it wasn't long before the food came. Their table was soon loud with chatter, and laughter, and stealing chips from someone else's plate when they weren't looking.

Grandma Iris leaned in close. 'So,' she said.

'So,' Evie replied.

She found that she couldn't speak.

She couldn't find the right words to tell Grandma Iris just how much her gifts meant. Not just to her, but to Ryan and Isabelle, and all the magical creatures they'd met along the way. There had been excitement, and thrills. But there had been special moments, when she'd just enjoyed being caught up in the big, amazing marvel of being in the world. Because of Grandma Iris' gifts, the things that seemed impossible had become possible. There were no words big enough to say thank you for that.

'So,' Grandma Iris said again. She
looked right into Evie's eyes, and some of
what Evie had been thinking must have
been written there, or maybe Grandma Iris
had a bracelet for reading minds, because

she said, 'It wasn't all magic. It was you too, Evie. Not everyone would have shared with their friends, or learned from their mistakes the way you have. It wasn't the bracelets making you special. It was the girl you are that did that.'

Grandma Iris patted Evie's hand. 'You can tell me all about it this holidays. We've got days and days to talk about it all.'

'Will you build a sandcastle with us, Grandma?' Lily interrupted suddenly, from across the table.

'Wild horses couldn't stop me. Hey! Is that a unicorn?' Grandma Iris said, pointing over Lily's shoulder.

Lily spun around. While her back was

turned, Grandma Iris swiped one of her chips.

'Oi!' Lily said. 'Well, at least I haven't got a spider in my hair,' she said airily.

'What?' Grandma's hands, and eyes, shot up to her head.

Lily swiped one of Grandma's chips.

Evie giggled. She was right where she wanted to be. With her funny, brilliant family, and her fantastic friends, at the start of a summer adventure.

And she still had a bracelet with two more days' worth of magic.

She felt that nothing was impossible, not today.

Evie and friends

Evie

Full name: Evie Hall

Lives in: Sheffield

Family: Mum, Dad, younger sister Lily

Pets: Chocolate Labrador Myla and cat Luna

Favourite foods: rice, peas and chicken – lasagna – and chocolate bourbon biscuits!

Best thing about Evie: friendly and determined!

Isabelle

Full name: Isabelle Carter

Lives in: Sheffield

Family: Mum, Dad, older sister Lizzie

Favourite foods: sweet treats – and anything spicy!

Best thing about Isabelle: she's the life and soul of the party!

Ryan

Full name: Ryan Harris

Lives in: Sheffield

Family: lives with his mum, visits his dad

Pets: would love a dog …

Favourite foods: Marmite, chocolate – and anything with pasta!

Best thing about Ryan: easy-going, and fun to be with!

What's your
Magic Bracelet ★ ★ ♥ ✧ ♥ perfect holiday?

Take this quiz to find out
which holiday would be perfect for you!

What's your favourite way to spend a day?

A. ❑ A long country walk.
B. ❑ Sightseeing – museums, art galleries, the lot!
C. ❑ Relaxing in the sun with a good book, then a dip in the pool.

What's your favourite food?

A. ❑ Barbecue – everything tastes better when you cook it outside!
B. ❑ I fancy going out to try sushi.
C. ❑ Good old fish 'n' chips for me!

I'm best at ...

A. ❑ Being creative, and mending things. I'm always up for a new challenge!

B. ❑ I'm an ace at map reading and negotiating public transport.

C. ❑ I'm a great swimmer.

And what's your favourite animal?

A. ❑ A dog – to race around with all day and snuggle up with all night!

B. ❑ I love cats – happy to do their own thing.

C. ❑ It's got to be dolphins!

Mostly A
Your perfect holiday is: *camping!*

Mostly B
Your perfect holiday is: *city break!*

Mostly C
Your perfect holiday is: *beach!*

Can you find all the words?

EVIE   ISABELLE
GOLDEN   PARROT
MAGIC   RYAN
FAMILY   BRACELET
HOLIDAY   FRIENDS

A	T	Z	R	G	Y	C	W	F	Z
B	V	O	S	Y	I	I	H	R	D
T	R	C	R	G	A	O	W	I	W
A	H	A	A	R	L	N	N	E	J
H	K	M	C	I	A	Y	J	N	Y
V	O	H	D	E	X	P	R	D	L
I	S	A	B	E	L	L	E	S	I
U	Y	E	V	I	E	E	N	S	M
N	E	D	L	O	G	A	T	P	A
W	P	V	D	R	C	S	N	K	F
M	E	M	U	Z	X	Z	N	E	J

A	T	Z	R	G	Y	C	W	F	Z
B	V	O	S	Y	I	I	H	R	D
T	R	C	R	G	A	O	W	I	W
A	H	A	A	R	L	N	N	E	J
H	K	M	C	I	A	Y	J	N	Y
V	O	H	D	E	X	R	R	D	L
I	S	A	B	E	L	L	E	S	I
U	Y	E	V	I	E	E	N	S	M
N	E	D	L	O	G	A	T	P	A
W	P	V	D	R	C	S	N	K	F
M	E	M	U	Z	X	Z	N	E	J

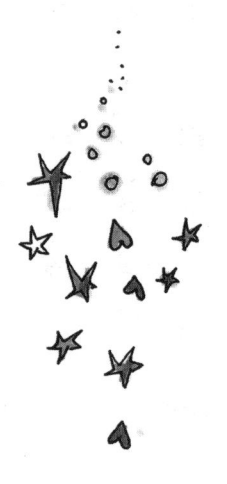

Jessica Ennis-Hill grew up in Sheffield with her parents and younger sister. She has been World and European heptathlon champion and won gold at the London 2012 Olympics and silver at Rio 2016. She still lives in Sheffield and enjoys reading stories to her son every night.

You can find Jessica on Twitter **@J_Ennis**, on Facebook, and on Instagram **@jessicaennishill**

Jessica says: *'I have so many great memories of being a kid. My friends and I spent lots of time exploring and having adventures where my imagination used to run riot! It has been so much fun working with Elen Caldecott to go back to that world of stories and imagination. I hope you'll enjoy them too!'*

Elen Caldecott co-wrote the Evie's Magic Bracelet stories with Jessica. Elen lives in Totterdown, in Bristol – chosen mainly because of the cute name. She has written several warm, funny books about ordinary children doing extraordinary things.

You can find out more at www.elencaldecott.com